The Heart Keeps Faulty Time

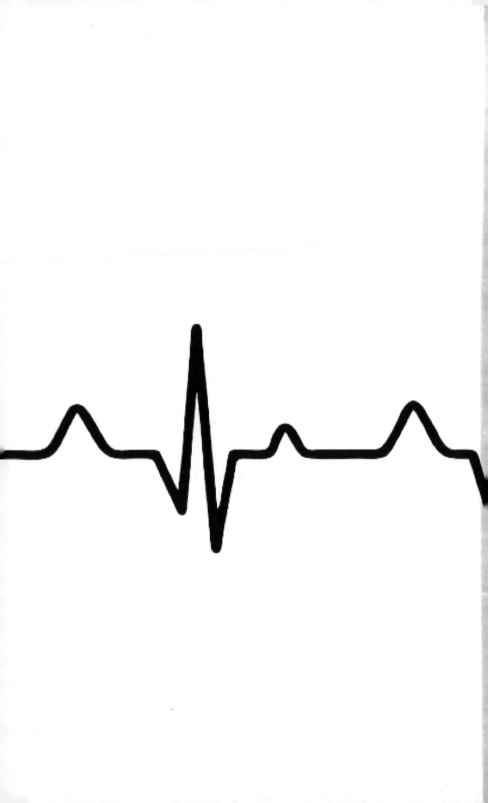

The Heart Keeps Faulty Time

stories

Siân Griffiths

DURHAM, NORTH CAROLINA

The Heart Keeps Faulty Time

Library of Congress Cataloging-in-Publication Data
Griffiths, Siân
The Heart Keeps Faulty Time: stories / by Siân Griffiths
p. cm.
ISBN-13: 978-1-949344-11-0

Book design by Spock & Associates

S P O C K

Cover art by Gwendolyn Myers

Published by

BULL CITY PRESS
1217 Odyssey Drive
Durham, NC 27713

www.BullCityPress.com

Contents

The Key Bearer's Parents

We were good parents. We know people assume otherwise when they see our wide ties and honking red noses, but we were. We took that job seriously. We told our son that he could be anything he wanted to be, just like you're supposed to. Yes, we could see his embarrassment when we showed up for Career Day. We saw how he threw the basketball into the field as our tiny car pulled in so that his friends would look away. Though we were happy clowns, smiles broader and wider than any lips, the disappointment underneath our makeup was easy to read.

"It's fine," we said, fitting on our oversized shoes and adjusting the flowers in our hats. We told ourselves that he would get over it.

On the news, the talk was all nuclear war and how to avoid it. The broadcasts filled with the whole "key bearer" plan. Ethicists argued that war would be less likely if some kind of key were implanted in a person's heart. What president wouldn't pause if he had to stab the bearer to drop that bomb? The president, they said, must be the first to bloody his hands.

We sheltered our boy from all of that talk. Children should have aspirations. They should believe in their own future, if nothing else. We gave him tennis lessons, enrolled him in Spanish and pottery classes. He would tell us what his friends had signed up for, and we would run to the Parks office to sign him up as well. Sure, we showed him our own trade secrets—how to walk in hoop-belted trousers, how to paint a face that reduces you to a single emotion—but he wasn't really interested, and we wouldn't hold him back. We only wished his aspirations weren't so heavily laced with judgment against our own.

Fine, though, fine. While Congress continued its endless debates, we sent him to prep school and on to private college, exhausting all we'd saved, then taking a series of loans. We worried over his talk of graduate school, an MBA, and how on earth we would afford it. He wanted to be a professional, he said.

"A professional what?" we never asked. He'd decide that in time. We pictured him leaning over a mahogany desk, sleeves rolled and tie abandoned, late at night when everyone else in the office had left. We pictured his boss patting him on the back one morning and telling him he'd made partner or would be the new CFO.

The summer before his junior year, our son came home, played tennis with his friends in the morning and drank bourbon in the afternoon. No one should be so angry while wearing white shorts. In Congress, the idea of burying the key to nuclear annihilation, like treasure in a human chest, was gaining traction.

"What about a trip to the fair?" we asked. "We'll get elephant ears, ride rides. You always loved the tilt-a-whirl."

"Fuck the tilted world," he growled, impressed with his own clever wordplay, as he once again grabbed his racquet and headed out. Make-upless and uncostumed, relegated to the parked car, we watched him play. He scowled through the chain link, each serve fueled by rage. His forehands brutal, his overheads unapologetically smashed into the stomachs of his opponents.

"Perhaps he'll be a tennis coach?" we whispered. That at least would bring some kind of joy, right? A brand of entertainment?

When he decided not to go back to school, there was the electrician apprenticeship, and we thought, ok, no more college, no being a professional, but blue collar is fine. Our last electrician complained that he could only charge $58 an hour here when he got $92 in California ten years ago—all of which seemed hopeful enough. It was more than we'd ever seen clowning, but that's life in the arts for you. Our boy was practical. Maybe he'd had too much time with his snobby friends? We thought maybe his anger had spent itself out.

When the bill passed, even the electrician thing evaporated. *Yes,* they voted, a bipartisan victory, and called for a volunteer to fill the key bearer's post. Good benefits, they claimed, a life of luxury, so long as you were willing to be murdered at any moment.

We snorted at the nightly news. "Who," we said to one another, "would ever volunteer for such a thing?" The whims of politics, the fickle world? Be serious. Life was too precious. If we knew anything, we knew that.

Alone in the room, his door locked as always, our son was already filling out the online application. And now that he's been selected, fished from their pool of thousands of applicants, we know we should be happy for him. He has what he wanted: steady pay, gourmet food on demand, a home in the nation's mansion, all the time in the world for tennis.

Still, we can't help wondering: Is it easier to kill a man who never laughs? This boy of ours. . . . We wish we could paint a smile on his face, teach him to spread cheer. We wonder how he ever grew so joyless. We tried to show him better, right to the end.

"Money," we said, "is the root of all evil."

He only looked at us, mustering the closest thing to a grin he's ever possessed.

"Yes," he said, "but a man needs roots."

Persistence of Geese

You awake to find a goose lying on your belly, another kind of nest. Webbed feet press into your vulnerable middle, and lofted down whispers against your skin with each breath, yet her body rests lighter than the thought of her body.

It isn't until her neck arcs toward you and she takes your nose in her bill that you realize this has all happened before. You try the usual tricks: stroke the wings and offer the stale oyster crackers you keep close at hand for these occasions. Still, her small teeth embed in your cartilage, and her moist tongue rests against your nostril, and her impenetrable black eye, which looks like a bead on your mother's last dress, peers into your eye.

You pull on your jeans, your sneakers, button her under your overcoat, and visit the butcher who has helped you out of these messes before. He is able to remove all but the head, sending you home with paper-wrapped cutlets for the deep freeze.

The packages are surprisingly heavy, as is the bodyless head. You will grow used to these weights, like so many others: the snout dangling from your left ear lobe, the muzzle, an epaulet on your shoulder, the lips around each toe.

You Were Raised by a Dragon.

What Was It Like?

Did her scales prickle or slide on your skin? Did her tongue flicker against your cheek like a kiss? Was it hot? Was it cold? Did she coddle you? Did she tell you about the knight, of the darkness he brings on his stout horse? Of what did the milk from her dragon breast taste—honeysuckle or pear, meat or maggot? Was it sweet or bitter? At what age did it sour? Did she give you dragonback rides? Did she encourage you to take candy from strangers? How about meth? When she holds you, do you feel love or terror or did you earlylearn how easily those feelings intertwine? Did she tell you how the villagers love knights best? How they tweet and Instagram their favorites, #therightknight, #knightieknight, #diredragonsdoom, #therewillbeblood? Did she light cigarettes with her breath? Did she press those lit cigarettes to your skin? Blow smoke in your face? Did she demand your smoke in return? Was your curfew strict? Did she comfort or discomfort you? Did she leave a night-light burning or did you rely on the yellow gleam from her unclosing eye when the nightmares came? Did she dip napkins in water glasses to rub away your stains or did she leave you dirty? Did you fend for yourself? Did she show you how to take your terror and make it live elsewhere? Did she show you how to flick your tail, to spread your wings, to gnash your teeth? Did she teach you to listen for hooves thundering on turf? for clanking armor? For the snorting breath of a tired animal carrying too much weight, spurred on by the cruel rowels never mentioned in fairy tales? Did she tell you about the lance, how it comes and comes? Did she tell you that there never was a princess? Did you take it to heart, or, at the end of it all, did only the tip of the lance penetrate?

Let's face facts: you're a middle-aged man with no life skills aside from your ability to choose an exceptional pair of slippers. You have a paunch and a bald spot and a mole on your left hand and you haven't had a girl-friend since high school, and that one only lasted two-and-a half-days, give or take ten minutes.

That's not entirely true. You're in your mid-thirties and on the pasty side and you may not have a paunch exactly because in truth you're too skinny even to carry a paunch, but your belly has gone slack and you would have man boobs if you were capable of carrying enough weight to have man boobs and your hair is more thinning than bald per se, but it's all coming. That future self. He stares at you in the mirror each day, only a little under the surface, like the seed of a weed you can't kill.

You want to write away death and age. You hold a pencil in your hand. No, you lay your hands on the keyboard. No, it's both: one and then the other. Your feet slide into the slippers like fish into coral, as if there is safety in darkness, but the pencil is octagonal and it bites into your fingers and the keys all snap back at you when you poke them.

One truth remains: not everyone can select a good pair of slippers. Too often, people are lured in by ephemera: claws, puppy-dog heads, thick rolls of fur. They fail to think about the morning paper lying in its plastic bag at the end of a wet sidewalk. They forget Snickers, who won't meow to go out, who has not left the house voluntarily in seven years, whose paws must be saved from the indignity of snow, who each morning you must carry to the sandy square under the eave of the shed to find his spot because you are not—not ever—dealing with cat litter. No, most people look only at a slipper's surface decor, thinking of easy chairs and kitchen floors and being cozy and cute.

You, however, are a novelist—a romance novelist—and you need to think about your feet. Your doctor, a young guy who wears wire-framed glasses to look like he knows something, said it's poor circulation that makes your toes cold. You asked if that meant your heart wasn't doing his job. He said probably not but who knows and sent you to the desk to make your co-pay. You haven't gone back. You know what you need to know: good slippers. Cold toes make for crappy love scenes, and that's a fact.

But you've been betrayed. Two months into this new pair, and a hole has formed. You can feel it circling your toe, strangling it like a dental-floss noose, inconsiderate of the fact that you have a deadline to meet.

Your notes on the project:

```
Esmerelda  Von  Clair,  heiress  and  confirmed
shopaholic,  has  been  kidnapped  by  the  evil
communist/fascist/atheist/leftist/terrorist
(TBD), Dr. Vincent Dondertrout, and is being held
for ransom. The U.S. gov't has selected elite spy
Jack Spratt (he'll never forgive his parents for
that one) to infiltrate Dondertrout's lair and
rescue the heiress. The problem is...
```

...that there is no problem yet. Jack Spratt's too good. He'll spring her in minutes. You can't think of a hitch, not with the toe-noose situation. And then there's Esmerelda. Sure, she's a classic babe, but her voice keeps coming out all wrong. It squeaks like old bubble gum against your teeth. You just can't see Spratt going for such an epic twit, even as a casual lay.

Really, it would be better if he were a widower. Your readers always like the widowers best, a fact your editor will remind you of as soon as she gets one whiff of this whole spy angle. *What are you thinking with this genre change, anyway? Have you forgotten who your audience is?* she'll ask in her email, and you'll imagine her voice all high and pinched to show that she knows—is fully and completely aware—that you have lost your mind. Spratt's too dangerous and unpredictable. He's not a husband type, not a comfort man. Any female reader worth her salt will instantly recognize him as a flight risk.

You get up and pace. Pacing always helps. Walking moves the blood around, gets it back into your head where it needs to be, rather than rushing to the rescue of your poor besieged toe. You can feel the floor right through your double-welded rubber-core synth-mesh triple-ply soles. The memory foam in this pair flattened almost as soon as you got them—it should have been called goldfish foam for all the memory it had.

If your life were a book, you think, your editor would be calling about now to remind you of your deadline. Unlike your real editor, the book version would be obstreperously male, with a voice like a gravel road in summer; the unsettling dust of his words would float in the air long after the rushing voice was gone. Your editor would tell you that he needs your copy by Tuesday, that he's waited far too long already.

Of course, in fiction as in life, the deadline wouldn't get you writing. Instead, it would send you outside, the fictional outside, get you to clear your head, collect the mail maybe, anything to avoid the silence coming from your keyboard. There, you'd trip on a dog that you'd failed to notice—a yappy little kick-dog that looked like an overgrown hamster with a bad perm, charging down the sidewalk and into your yard at the end of one of those mile-long retractable leashes that you always see as a sure sign of irresponsible pet ownership, proof that it's the dog who wears the pants in that relationship. It'd yip when you stepped on it (do those dogs have any other response?), and you'd start to growl back, and only then, at that precise moment, would you look up and see a woman. She wouldn't look like much: mid-fifties, gray. But one glance at her eyes, and you'd know there was more to her than just looks.

She wouldn't apologize. Why would she? You were the one who wasn't looking. Instead, she'd say something daffy like, "Boy, Charles really loves you," even though the hamster dog wouldn't be paying you any attention, even though the hamster dog would be wrapped ten times around your mailbox post on its absurd leash. But you'd set up a date for coffee anyway, and the whole incident would propel you back to your keyboard where, in a flurry of inspiration, you'd write exactly the kind of novel you always write, the ones they've come to expect from you, the ones that provide enough of an advance to pay the very real bills that are probably at this moment waiting in the very real mailbox. The bills that are already past due.

Your real editor doesn't have a remotely gravelly voice. Or perhaps she does, but you only communicate through email, and if the picture hovering next to her messages can be believed, she's all mouse hair and scarves, everything done up to affect some sort of confidence that has never and will never leak into those startled eyes.

You get up and carry Snickers outside. There is no woman, no hamster dog. No one's out there but that homeschooled kid across the road. He's too old to be sitting in the dirt with a stick in his hand, but damned if that isn't just what he's doing. The kid has to be eight or nine at least. He should be on a bike or a skateboard or throwing a ball into the air to practice catching it, only his arms look too much like overcooked spaghetti to suggest he'd be much good at any kind of sport.

As Snickers wraps his purring, vibrating body around your legs, as his eyes plead with you to let him back into the safety of the house even though he has yet to take his requisite dump, you rack your brain for the kid's name: Daniel? Jonathan? Michael? No, it's something loopy. The kind of name that guarantees you'd have to homeschool the kid if he's to have any hope of surviving elementary school. Algernon? Louis? Sinclair? No. You know you've heard it—you remember thinking it'd be perfect for one of your novels, where you could assign it to the kind of strapping male who could survive the burden of his name, who would in fact be made sensitive by it, more sympathetic to women and small animals—but whatever the kid's name is, it has vanished from your memory.

You let Snickers back in and rummage the cupboards for cheese puffs or fire-roasted tomato snack crackers, even though you know you ran out yesterday. You told yourself then: no more cheese puffs until you have a solid draft. "BICHOK," you told yourself—"Butt In Chair, Hands On Keyboard"—but what seemed like a good incentive to work yesterday is now revealing itself as more than usually shortsighted. Working without snack crackers? What the crap were you thinking? Comfort is the heart and soul of the creative impulse.

You open the fridge and rummage to the back to find a single, solitary gherkin failing to float in the pickle jar. You stab at it with a fork, but it breaks in two, so you resort to dumping the brine over your hand, trying to catch the pickle on its egress, only to watch it slide through your fingers in the flood of brine and disappear down the disposal where you consider, briefly, fishing it out before washing your hands and returning to your desk and the silence of the keyboard.

You wonder if the kid is still out there playing in the dirt with the stick. What is he writing in the dirt anyway? What could be so compelling? You stare at your own uncompelling document another five full minutes without typing a thing before you simply have to know.

The day has gotten surprisingly warm. You certainly don't need the added heat of the 100% polyspun furtastic pro-faux fleece that's tufted around your feet—excepting, of course, the one toe sticking lewdly from its hole. Indeed, the boy is still sitting there. His freckles are dark in the sunlight. He has more freckles than you have ever seen on one face, so many that his face seems more freckled than unfreckled. You wonder if he can properly be called "white," though what else would you call him? "Pinto?" "Skewbald?" You shuffle up and stand there, looking at the circles he's insistently reinscribing. He looks up at you, eyes all squinty and piggish in the sun.

"You the guy who writes them titty books," he tells you.

It takes you a moment to process this: the fact that he has spoken to you, the fact that he knows more of your life that you do of his. You collect your dignity to attempt an imperious look.

"They are most certainly not titty books," you say.

You can only imagine your editor's response to that. The word "titty" has never appeared in a single one of your books. Your readers would abandon you on the spot. No, they favor "breasts" and, in certain key moments, "heaving bosoms." They allow well-endowed chests that rise and fall as the heroine pants under the gentle hands of the widowed man struggling to overcome the memory of his dead wife so that he might love again. The woman he caresses strives in turn to show him that she, yes, she, is precisely the cure he needs to release himself from the haunting power of his past devotion. Her fingertips and hers alone know the language that will speak to his soul and unlock him from the prison in which he never until that moment realized he was bound.

"Well, Mama says they're titty books and that I'm not to speak to you."

"Does she even read? My books?" you ask, adding *my books* as an afterthought to save the question from being too brazen.

"Mama reads the Bible."

"Well," you say. "Of course she does."

That seems to end the conversation. The boy nods, as if there was no sarcasm in your tone, as if you sought merely to confirm his mother's sainted status as the neighborhood Mother Theresa or Tammy Faye Bakker or whomever it is she holds up as an icon.

The boy squints at you again. It really is a beautiful day out: mid-sixties, a light breeze, the few clouds moving as leisurely across the sky as sheep in a field. Which is, of course, part of the problem. Writing is best on rainy days, so long as there's no lightning to threaten your surge suppressors. What you need is a nice cold snap. What you need is a mild front to come in, carrying inspiration and a light drizzle.

The boy says, "Your slipper is broke."

"Thank you, Dr. Watson."

"It's too hot for them kind of slippers. Your feet'll be all sweaty and smell like cheese."

Jesus. Doesn't this kid know anything? Doesn't this kid know there are some things you just don't say? You peer down at him.

"You know, freckles are supposed to be the sign of the devil. The mark where the devil came to nurse. He must have nursed off you like crazy. You must be all full of devil's milk."

That sets the boy back. He tucks his chin and blows his cheeks out like a balloon trying to inflate itself. You feel a momentary pride in having gotten him to shut up for a moment, to let him know what it feels like to have something wrong said to him. You can see that the boy is considering your words seriously. He's taking them in, internalizing. Tears are pricking in the corners of his eyes. You did that: made an innocent kid into the cow of Satan. You should've known this kid has no sense of irony. You of all people should know that words create their own realities. Your feet are sweaty. He wasn't wrong about that.

"Listen, kid," you say, "it's just a story. No one really believes that."

You wish you had some potato chips.

"I wish I had me some potato chips," the boy says.

You look at him sternly for a full minute, making sure he has good warning to stay out of your head. "I need to work," you say.

Your writing desk was your grandmother's vanity. You've written here since you were fourteen years old and your mother decided it was time to move you and your extensive Lego collection out of her living room. You first tried your hand at writing fantasy novels, only to realize you couldn't write a fight scene worth your ass. It is wholly inappropriate as a writing desk: too narrow, too cramped. The varnish is stripped where your grandmother spilled a bottle of perfume, years ago, when she was courting the man before the man who would be your grandfather. You once thought the mark was perfect for a writing desk: what better inspiration than that Rorschach of a stain? Is *stain* even the proper word? Can you use it to mean the mark of something removed, rather than something lingering?

Your neck hurts. The light bulb in the desk lamp is all wrong. Too blue or too white. You bought one of those fluorescent bulbs that promise to last forever, and now it is your great fear that it will and you won't have any excuse to replace it with something warmer. You long for it to burn out. Is *burn out* the right phrase for these bulbs? You realize you have no idea. You realize that you have no idea how it even works. The old ones made sense: vacuums and filaments, every day burning themselves toward destruction. Those old bulbs were something you could relate to.

You bought this new one in a home-supply store when your last normal bulb went in a flash and a pop. Around you, men in overalls bought lumber and screws and made complicated choices about plumbing fixtures. They prepared to install elaborate outdoor lighting while you were baffled by the simple choice of bulb. A woman in a red vest had approached you. The name stitched into her vest read "George" and she was too beautiful to work in a home-supply store, though you suppose in retrospect that bar was rather low. In a nail salon or a sushi restaurant, perhaps she would have only been average. Perhaps in those places her green eye makeup would've appeared garish or her bangs teased too high. In the home-supply store, though, she was a backlit angel, the long fluorescents of the store illuminating her hair.

She asked if you needed help, and you said "yes" with all your heart. "Yes," you want to say again, even now. "Yes, every day." You wanted to say, "Come home with me and we'll eat bologna on the embarrassment of a couch that I've wanted so long to replace and we'll watch the small brown birds out the front window. You will be my muse. I will write books and books and books about you."

Instead, you said, "I need a bulb." At which point, she handed you this one, too blue or too white, and left you.

You walk back out into the sunshine. The boy has not moved.

"Still no potato chips?" you say.

He shrugs. "Any luck writing your titty book?"

You shrug. You sit next to the boy and notice that the circles he's drawing might themselves be large breasts, small areolae and smaller nipples, nipples so small that they scarcely seem to be circles at all, only dots.

"What's your name?" you ask, surprising yourself.

"Percival."

"Not Jeremiah? Not Ezekiel? I thought your mom was a Christian."

"Mama is not my mom."

You stare at the boy as if his freckles might explain this mystery. As if by connecting those dots, you could connect these.

"My folks is dead," he says. "Mama is my aunt."

"You only get one mom, kid," you say.

Spratt would never stand for any of this, you know. Not the motherless boy on the curb. Not the coldness of the light bulb. Not the lack of potato chips. Not the dusty-rose couch that's brown along the back from your dead uncle's hair grease. Spratt inhabits another world altogether, a world that only sometimes and slantwise resembles yours. You can sense him there, leaning casually at the edge of all of this, eating one of those rich person's crackers spread with food beyond any you've ever tasted, caviar or foie gras, and staring at you pityingly.

You've seen the boy's mama-aunt before now, juggling groceries from her faded blue Plymouth or shoving a lawn mower across the grass. She's a large woman with red hands and the kind of nose that brooks no argument. The instant you saw her you felt that she'd never had sex and that she disapproved of anyone else who'd been luckier than her in that regard, but the boy had seemed to stand in contradiction to that until now.

Before now, however, you have not seen her from the vantage point of a curb with her glowering over you, six foot tall if an inch. You imagine from the turn of her mouth that you are in trouble, but then you realize it is the boy who is in trouble, and that you are the cause. Her blue eyes spark against her beet-colored skin. She is maybe five, ten years older than you, and her skin appears to have been sanded, but, rather than smoothing her out, this apparent sanding has made it rough. You wonder if she, too, was once as freckled as the kid, and if her freckles spread and grew until her whole face merged into that one motley color.

"You coming in for lunch?" she says to the boy, and in that moment, despite the fierce purse of her lips, her loneliness opens like the petals of a flower unfurling. It was right there inside her all the time, but her words rolled it out before you. You see it all: the absence where her sister had been, the boy who won't stay inside. You see the long days in the kitchen and then in the living room with a soap opera on. You see that sad little bed that's never made because why bother? What man will ever see it? You see in this woman what you always should have seen: your reader. She is the woman you have been waiting for all your life, to woo, to comfort, to offer solace, for whom to build people too beautiful for this life, people who never burp or sweat or fart when they bend to pick up the morning paper, people who only suffer beautiful sicknesses that make them thin and full of pathos, people who rescue those who need to be rescued. People nothing like yourself or the boy or his aunt. You and her, so focused on making your way that you scarcely have time to look up and find one another across the street, let alone tether each other against all the invisible forces that batter you both.

"Come with me," you say to the woman. "I'll fix you both some lunch."

You want her to join you more than you've ever wanted anything. You know that your last book is hidden right now in the drawer of her bedside table where she fears the boy will find it. You want to know this woman, to understand.

She looks at you with those small blue eyes, suspicious of your motivations. You are a grown man who writes titty books and sits with small children on the roadside.

"You need to work."

The way she says it makes it unclear if she considers writing as work enough, whether she's implying that you should go and get a real job—selling hats, perhaps. You've always liked that word: *haberdasher*.

"Come on," you repeat. "There's bologna."

She looks at you a good long while as you sit there wearing your new-but-broken slippers, your sweaty toe pointing out like a stubby little penis. You try to smile a reassuring smile, but you can tell by the feel of your cheeks that it's coming out all wrong. She looks at you until it's clear she's letting you know with this look that she knows the devil's work is at play. She huffs a breath, clutching the boy's hand in hers to fetch him home. She jerks him behind her, hurting and protecting him. As you watch them, the boy casts one last look back to you before he disappears behind the door. You won't get to talk to him again any time soon. Really, what else did you expect?

Maybe another time, you tell yourself. Maybe not. For now, you'll go back in. You've got some thoughts for Esmerelda. You've had a light bulb, an idea regarding the girl's dead parents. You realize now that she has an aunt who resides in New Hampshire, a quiet woman who raised the girl as her own. Desperate for help in finding her niece, the aunt will call Spratt. She'll reach out for him. You were right all along. Esmerelda was never the right lover for a man like him. For a while, she might confuse him with her beautiful sensuality, but the aunt's patient and quiet yearning will prevail.

You take a last breath of the fresh air. It really is a glorious day, even if it is all wrong for writing. It's a shame, you think, that the woman wouldn't come along, but then, readers never do, do they? Not willingly. They slide away like fish on any new current. You have to catch them in your own invisible flow of words, pull them along the way they think they're swimming, buoy them and tickle under their fins until they arrive with you at the inevitable end, the place you couldn't avoid, the place neither of you knew you were going.

An Imaginary Number

for Gwendolyn

That night, she danced with aliens. They spoke to her in math. In school, she was learning multiplication tables and isolation; she understood whispers as sound waves measuring the distance between planets. School math was rote. Alien math worked on another logic, requiring no memory. Their three-step time altered her heart's beat.

Though the waltz was a one-time thing, it was an instant that stretched its roots through her past and budded tendrils into every moment of her future. Just as in English *cleave* can mean parting or coming together, their language allowed one time, simultaneously, to be all time. Or perhaps it was simply the nature of moments to be both fleeting and forever. There was no telling.

The dance tempo was determined by her body, which unlike theirs was bound to the earth and the moon and the rotations of the sun, a concept of time born in a body brought up by those celestial bodies. Each step marked a moment between birth and death, between here and there, between alien and familiar. She knew love from her parents, though work took them daily. These new beings took her hands in their appendages. They matched their rhythms to hers, and then allowed rhythm to evolve, solving an equation. Down the hall, her parents stirred, though the music in the room was soundless.

What called the aliens to her from across the stars? She did not know. When they returned from whence they came, she was no longer one lonely girl but, rather, a girl for whom loneliness had become an imaginary number, a girl whose understanding stretched to contain galaxies, a girl whose limbs, even now, contain that once-waltz.

Everyone Fails

Everyone fails the first time. It's what Tucker told you, morning after morning, as you and he sipped coffee from the same old mugs, preparing for another day of training. A flight pattern would be a little crooked, or your X-ray vision wouldn't permeate that particular thickness of steel, or the simulated baby rescued from the fire would have a slight cough. *If being a hero were easy,* he'd say, *everyone would do it.*

Packing the mug was dumb. It was fragile, breakable. It wasn't a stowed-bag kind of thing. But you told yourself you couldn't be your best on Styrofoam coffee. You told yourself that it'd done its time, and it was already chipped anyway, and you didn't care if it smashed. You told yourself a lot of things.

The truth is, you never intended to fail. Your training group spent the summer clearing pines, tossing them into the back of the rig with a flick of your fingers. You and Tucker raced farm kids in their souped-up trucks, letting them eat your dust on those hot gravel roads. With the strong track records of Gotham and Metropolis, no one looked to Idaho for heroes, but you were determined to show them why they should. Tucker suggested you rethink that, adopt a fake city, sharpen your look. You insisted that hometown was your *brand.*

Tucker had already tried out twice and refused to believe that the third time held any kind of charm. Sure, he could go freelance, but then you were reliant on tips for derring-dos. Go through the show, and you were in the union making union wages. You'd watched each of Tucker's seasons umpteen times, recorded off NBC, trying to understand why they hadn't taken him. Lean as he was, he faded perfectly into his alter-ego look. Glasses on, and he was a nerd, a wimp, a background guy no one noticed slipping into the phone booth. He was someone out of *Queer Eye*, or the *Jeopardy!* contestant everyone forgot the instant he'd won his hundred thousand. Loosen the tie, though, and he was a lean, mean, ass-kicking machine. The panel of heroes had to have seen that.

You wonder now, as you sip and sip, if he was too alter ego, too middle America. *No one wants a hero who's relatable*, Tucker said. In hindsight, you could have ordered custom tights, had your hair done at a salon, consulted with a graphic designer on a logo, or Christ, even had your artsy sister mock something up, but honestly, this was supposed to be about skill. You chose to wear that summer's faded yoga pants and oversized cotton tee, pit-stained and rank, under a worn flannel.

You don't know if you are more aggravated at your lack of vision (superpowered in every sense but the figurative) or at theirs. You saw it in the women's looks from the moment you entered: disgust. The men (super-, bat-, aqua-, spider-) were merely bemused. The women, though? Their faces said it all. They'd worked too hard to get any kind of respect, and here you were, a mockery. It didn't matter that you'd aced every test they threw your way. You would be judged by the same standards they'd had to pass. Diana Prince asked your cup size. Natalia Romanova ran a tape around your hips and frowned at the number under her thumb.

Who exactly do you think you are? Did she speak the words, or was it her thoughts you heard? Sometimes, it is hard to know, particularly with that kind of proximity. You had thought you'd be Cougra or the Mountain Lioness, something lithe, inspired by the big cats that slunk from the woods to blend with the tawny ripened wheat. You were to be the one they never saw coming. Now, you have no idea who you are.

You think of Tucker and his endless reps, bench-pressing semi trucks, flexing afterward, hoping this time the muscles would bulge enough to tear his shirt. You reminded him about scrawny Peter Parker. Tucker said he was the exception that proved the rule. You shot back with Dare Devil, the old rules were shifting, the old prejudices were breaking down. Tucker: *Keep telling yourself that.*

"We'll let you know your results in six to eight weeks," Bruce said, but his eyes and the camera were already on the next candidate. The next candidate's legs.

So here you sit, back in the humming hotel room with the old coffee mug you'd packed for luck because sometimes all the superpowers in the world are not enough; though, as it turns out, neither are lucky mugs. Your mother bought it as a gift when you were five, filled it with cinnamon Jelly Bellies. A little sweet, a little spicy: your favorite. You cradle it, hot in your hands, plain and white except for your initial, a single *S* in large block font, like might appear on a football uniform (a man's sport, but it has never felt off-limits). The ceramic is chipped on the lip, exposed and unglazed where it touches you. Objects, you tell yourself, have the right to expose their vulnerabilities, just as people do, and if those vulnerabilities cause inconvenience or discomfort, whose right is it to label the thing flawed?

If you get the job, if they'll only give you a chance, you'll emblazon the old mug's *S* on your chest, pair it with ring-striped sleeves, lycra knee pants, and sneakers because you never could bear running in boots. So much about heroism needs a rethink.

You glance at your phone, not quite ready to text Tucker back, though you've watched it lighting to life every few minutes for the past few hours.

Six to eight weeks, you tell yourself, as if they haven't already given their answer, as if there's enough time for the world to change.

What Is Solid

A man sits on his porch, pipe in hand, blowing smoke rings. Then, as he puffs, a smoke ring floats, levels, and hangs itself over his head like a halo. The man waves his hand to make the smoke move along, only to rap his knuckle on the halo, which is no longer smoke but iron, and attached to the back of his skull by means of a thick, vertical wire.

The man drives to the hardware store. Beatrix, the proprietor, smiles and says, "Hello your holiness," as he walks in, his halo ringing the bell over the door. When he asks for wire cutters, Beatrix (her wicked smile!) says she's fresh out.

That's when he notices the growing heft of his shadow. He lifts his foot. Sure enough, his shadow is a thin, pliable, man-shaped sheet of lead.

"An ax?" he pleads, gesturing to his darker self, dense on the floor of the shop.

Beatrix only shakes her head.

The man begins to sweat but pats the sweat away with his white handkerchief, afraid to see what next might come from him. He hurries down the road, or tries to. Children, sick of their chalked boxes and colored ropes, begin jumping onto his shadow. They test their balance, see how long they can stand as the man hurries along, and watch the shadow spark as it drags.

He ignores the children, pretending they are not there even as he pulls their weight. Mainly, he is worried about what else they might do: he imagines a jumble of refrigerator magnets cluttering his halo, or a trail of streamers and tin cans, as if he were a honeymoon car.

When he stops to catch his breath, he realizes that he could *actually* catch his breath: it floats away, transparent balloons of his air. Invisible, except for the way they bend the light. He is transfixed by this: the lens of his exhalation. Has it always been this way? His head wobbles under the clumsy iron weight, as if it would nod, *yes, yes.*

Clockwork Girl at the Opera

Like many clockwork girls, I pass best clad in lace. I veil my head, shawl my shoulders. Though dogs sniff me out in a moment, people seldom notice my clicking. Men are easiest to fool. Let your laces slip, and you are as good as real—or so Charles suggests as he fingers my tucker. Within the cabriolet, the clattering hooves echo harshly as we hie ourselves to Haymarket. The cob on the cobbles. Charles's lips on my neck are soft as dove's wings. I dislike their flapping. The driver pulls us to a stop.

"Come, pet," Charles murmurs, "we must make our entrance."

Oh, the opera, that mechanism designed to provoke emotion. Charles adores a contralto. Tonight, we are bound for *La Cenerentola*. I wish he would take Elizabeth, but, he says, it does no good at all for a man to be seen with his own wife. She sleeps later these days, cries more often, grows fat. He can less and less stand the sight of her. She has not forgiven him for Peggy, her lady's maid, the most trusted servant in the house, now ruined and dismissed.

The clockwork clicks, the snag and spring of the metal arms. We live in an age of mad kings and miracles. I button my pelisse and step into the drizzle. Charles lays a hand on my hip, holding me to my part. His fingers slide publically (performance, performance). He tends a wisp of hair on my shoulder, allows his hand to brush my breast, then turns suddenly and smilingly towards the throng, as if caught in his act. He attempts a blush. Whispers of Peggy are moths flitting from the lips of the watching crowd, though no child will ever spring from my springs and coils. My stays will never be let out. I will not swell.

But look! Tonight, the entry is flanked by elephants, some kind of white rock. Their upturned trunks silently trumpet. They appear to dance in spite of their heaviness, as if the facts of being stone and elephants can be shed and forgotten, as if natural law could likewise cease and we might all live in a world that was nothing more or less than what we made it. Apply art to madness and the result is magic. Delightful! The music drifting through the air lends its own lightsomeness, a buoyancy that floats us until it feels that we are all just baskets suspended from balloons that hover amidst the unseen stars. The winds would have us dance.

We approach the standing crowd as they mingle outside the doors of the King's Theatre. A new king now that his father has passed. A new age. The show is running behind time. The gentlemen bristle and huff. Charles struts alongside me in patent leather boots, his greatcoat swinging at every stride. The brim of his hat shades his eyes, but they glint from within its shadow—whether in malice or delight it is impossible to say. He admires one sentiment as much as the other.

How Elizabeth carried on once Peggy confessed her condition! Charles, she said, had selected her maid out of spite. Her shouted words rebounded off walls, flying above and below stairs, traveling to every apartment. He could have had any other girl in the house—any one of them. Peggy was her own.

Over the damp wool, I smell blood on the air, mingling with the blackness of a West End night. A butcher's shop, I tell myself. Lazy drizzle drops itself from apparently clear skies, and I fear the malignant rust it carries. My brain tickles with its whirring, thoughts sliding past one another and failing to find order. Small, red puddles are scattered on the pavement, smeared by boot soles, drug by hems like oils by the brush. I make no sense of what's painted here, nor of the disordered skirts to which the drops lead me, the tiny black boots.

I feel as I sometimes do when Charles forgets to wind me. This is the problem with clockwork: dependence. At times, I've envied self-sustaining mechanisms: the heart, the lungs. I was made for night when the dark obscures my hinges and the subtle clacking of my machinery is cloaked in music. I am made for companionship, wound and used as convenient, left to adorn Elizabeth's dressing room when not. I'm told that when I am still, she hangs her soiled undergarments on my head, where they rest until collected.

A young lady screams. My head clicks right, chin slanted left, the appropriate expression of curiosity and dismay. Shocked murmurs become the new music as the quartet drops the pretense of their pavement concerto. A plot before the opera? The grand dame to my right raises an eyebrow to suggest that she suspects that this drama, too, is scripted. An amuse bouche to whet the appetite. Her raised eyebrow communicates that she finds it in poor taste.

In the thin glow of gaslight, the arm on the pavement is as pale as my own. Mud or freckles spatter a patternless design. On best quality muslin, set off with satin ribbons, the effect might have been pretty. On her pallid flesh, it is less so.

A gentleman nudges the arm with his brown boot, as if the inert girl were deplorable or diseased, which perhaps she is. Or was. Those of my kind are safer alternatives to the living. Nothing breeds or festers within me. One never knows what might be picked up from a common prostitute.

But I am guessing. Perhaps she is not such a one. She might have been an actress or a dressmaker or a daughter or a wife.

"Come now, ladies," says a red-haired, mustachioed man, the waxed tips jumping at his words. "Let's find a more suitable place for you, away from this . . ." He circles his hand in the air, as if to shoo unpleasantness away and return it to the dark. Away from this what? He does not finish his sentence. I wondered what language he considered and why he could find none suitable.

This? This girl dead in the gutter? This, I realize, is what is meant by *unspeakable*, and yet his unspeaking does not diminish her presence.

Whir, click, clack: an arm catches a tooth but skips its groove.

The mustachioed gentleman takes a plump young woman by her dimpled elbow. The strain on her dress seams suggests a fondness for pastry creams, and her lingering gaze gives evidence to an interest in other unsanctioned delights.

"My dear," she says, the yellow curls about her face bouncing with each syllable, "you must attend to her who is most in need."

"I fear the girl is beyond needing."

"A girl?" The woman's neck cranes to see beyond the screen of his tall hat. "So young?"

"Woman, perhaps. My dear, you upset yourself!" He pats her arm to tamp down her enthusiasm for the macabre, as if that delight resided in one's forearm. Those who constructed me could surely educate him otherwise.

I wonder if Prince George once touched his father's arm this way. Like me, the old man performed a part, fitted with robes and scepters only to be later called tyrant. Now he rots in a grave. His human brain was simply too frail for weighty pressures. It gave way, just as bones break when overtaxed. I wonder what words the prince shared with his father before realizing that language does not penetrate a mind unsprung.

I step away, moving towards the fallen one, curious myself. Girl or woman, the skin is certainly not aged. She should have had years before her. The scent of her blood is stronger here. It mixes with the oily scent of the Thames and a fresher breed of sourness: one of the gentlemen has been sick. Those lighter freckles mingle with the freckles of blood. The scent registers but does not affect me. I ascertain from the contents of his nasty pile that he dined on shellfish, white wine, potatoes, asparagus.

My makers might have neglected to give me this ability to recognize odors. I would have been none the worse for it, and it certainly presented them a challenge. But they were men of science, and in this enlightened age, they wanted to show the breadth of their genius. In each of my abilities, I am miraculous, they say, thereby proving the greater miracle of their own cleverness.

Charles chuckles under the streetlamp with an older man in a caped coat. Worn elbows intimate he neglects his wardrobe. No wife, then. No daughters. Even a housekeeper with influence enough might give a gentle word. His cravat, however, implies wealth, as does the fact that Charles speaks to him. Charles is not one to waste his time with just any man at the opera.

I shuttle my way forward, wefting through women, my feet moving quietly under my skirts so that my movements pass undetected. My dress is dark like the night, a somber color designed to burn red under the garish light of the chandeliers in the foyer. Here, in dimmer glow, I attract no notice as I move to the gutter's edge.

The servants whisper that Peggy serviced Elizabeth's own romantic needs long before the master bedded her. They say her tongue was quick and able between the mistress's thighs. They teased her about her fingers, so long and tender. They smirked in delight. The root of the mistress's outrage, they say, had more to do with these talents than with any work ethic or other skill that Peggy possessed.

I hear such rumors only when they forget that I am wound. None speaks to me directly, save Charles.

The girl's stomach—for girl she was, fifteen, perhaps sixteen—has been opened by a rough and bladed hand, a butcher's work. Steam curls its delicate fingers into the thin light, like her soul would crawl its way into some better place. Her blood moves sluggishly now, congealing in the cool air, but though its current is slow, still it trickles through her bodice and along the pavement to mingle with the gutter's foul soup as it makes its way towards river water.

I imagine someone touched her, and then wonder who that man might have been. I wonder if his whiskers pricked her thighs, if he shoved his fingers hard within her tender parts, if she was expected to feign enjoyment at these acts. He might have choked her with his man-hood; he might have battered and rammed her. Charles will do any of these, depending on his mood and his day at the office and his current feelings towards Elizabeth and whether she again has belabored the loss of Peggy. I am an entirely different kind of whipping boy on which he may expend his flog.

But this girl and I are nothing alike. She was only a thing.

Charles's booming laughter echoes off the stone walls. He claps his interlocutor on the shoulder and turns to look, his lips pulling into a sly but questioning smile. What am I doing lingering over a corpse?

Most of the men are involved in conversation or in ferrying their wives and daughters towards more wholesome sights. A wagon has been called for. "This will all soon be but a memory," says the mustachioed man, in a tone that suggests the hope that his wife will wipe it from her mind. The attention she devotes to the meat pie he procured suggests that he might not be entirely hopeless on that account. I feel I am winding down, though I should have hours yet to go.

This girl's heart beat once, moving her arms and legs. It allowed her to feel, even without anyone to ratchet her into consciousness. She had been able to live with no one's attention, if she chose. Removing a glove,

I kneel and stroke a coil of her entrails. It is sticky to the touch but firmer than I would have imagined. Her warmth is fading.

Charles lays a disapproving eye on me. I have just moments until he can make his way over if he hopes not to attract the attention haste would bring. The girl's eyes are lifeless. The blue, which must once have laughed and sparkled, is missing some vital component, though the lenses that compose them are still in their places. Their orbs are not displaced. The last of her blood is not entirely removed. I want to touch the girl's cheek. I want to know if it is as solid as her inner ropes, or whether her most exposed features were softer. My fingers are stained, though, and I would not wish to stain this girl. Or, rather, I do not wish to add my own marks to the spatters of blood and sick that freckle her sweet face.

Charles lifts me, his arm encircling me to shroud my body from view. His words rush over me, water over brook stones. I am unmoved. He clasps my wrist, dabbing my fingers with his handkerchief. They remain tinged. He draws my hand to his mouth, his gaze locked on mine as he places each finger, one by one, in his mouth and washes them with his tongue. His eyes are wet with desire. His flushed face is more eloquent than his hushed words. Tonight, he will have me reenact this in reverse, first sucking my fingers, then stabbing me with invisible knives, pulling forth the imagined surrogates of the vital parts I lack onto the bedspread, asking me to resist him while he has his way with me as the clockwork cunt clicks tight, independent of my will, subject only to his.

My thoughts are irrelevant. We live in an age of miracles.

Charles has clapped an arm around me once more.

"Come, pet," he says. I lean to his arm as he expects, as the scene requires, and we leave the girl's drained corpse.

My body could be wound endlessly, outliving Charles, Elizabeth, everyone. Just turn my key, and, as long as I am oiled and maintained, I will go on. That seems enough. A feat any mechanist might take pride in. Thought is as superfluous as scent.

Some say the soul rests in the mind, others the stomach. I have neither organ. My thoughts fly again and again to the girl. I envision her slopped on the wagon, bumping over the road stones on her way to a pauper's grave.

Animation was ample proof of the power of design. My makers gave me no pulse to quicken, no heart to break. Why, then, must I think and feel?

We find our seats. The curtain parts. Painted women (a maid, daughters) flaunt themselves center stage, their voices vibrating through my works. Charles, energized by soaring sound, clasps my cold hand. The function of music is to move those not regulated by escapement, but the drum, like the heart, keeps a faulty time.

Two Mermaids

The one I want kneels by Pike Place, hands on scaled hips, bare-breast-ed, bold; her eyes read the names writ in water. She's oblivious to the men in the market lazily tossing a sockeye salmon over iced perch, sev-ered crab legs, limp-footed geoducks.

The one I want is a far cry from this southern mermaid, landlocked on Broad Street in a shell constructed of rebar and stucco. I knock at the wrong mermaid's door because it's the closest I've got. She's just painted each of her green scales wet with clear nail varnish and a min-iscule brush. Her hair hangs chaste as a garment, her smiles are an es-pionage. She reveals nothing, chats politely, drawls her vowels. For the right price, she'll play muse. Scribes circle her, ears plugged with song, the smudge of red lipstick staining each collar. She would give her voice for legs.

I hand the wrong mermaid my throat, and in return, she pours espresso from a steaming pot. I take my seat at the edge of her flipper and sip a sip that has nowhere to go. I tell myself, all dreams are like this: cup-bound and scalding.

Paper Hats

The first one is simple. While his mother finishes adjusting her lipstick, the stranger in the orange tie shows the small boy the series of folds that transforms his mother's *Wall Street Journal* into both a boat and a hat.

That night, everything changes. Bo Bo Bear becomes Robin Hood. Then all his animals—an army of newsprint-topped Robins, filling his shelf. He folds sixteen more hat-boats the next afternoon. And so on. He unwraps a Doublemint Plen-T-Pack to fill the tub with a gum-wrapper fleet. He makes fifty-seven newspaper hats to have on hand for his next birthday party, though he does not know fifty-seven people to invite.

His mother sweeps the hats away in her fierce wind. *I hadn't even looked at that paper yet.*

For a while, he folds smaller hats, hiding them in unexpected places: behind the Saran Wrap, tucked inside the spare toilet roll. The almonds on the coffee table wear many hats.

The hats become more intricate: a fedora, a boater, the cap of an English fox hunter, the Kaiser's helmet. He watches for the battered Datsun and slips out to retrieve the paper before his mother notices its arrival. Afternoons, he walks to the library to study armory encyclopedias and women's fashion magazines. His mother now orders two papers, but he folds the second as well.

He makes rules for his hats: no scissors, no tape, no crayons, no paint. Nothing but the paper—itself and something more, all at once. His mother shrieks to find her second *Journal* folded and folded into the neck armor of an Imperial Japanese battle helmet. He apologizes by folding her next paper into a gift: a dainty pillbox circled with twisting clusters of roses, each stem delicately thorned.

Enough! she cries, and carries armload after armload to the hearth. He can't speak. The match flares, then dulls under the paper enough to raise hope before it flares again. He feels his heart, not beating in his chest, but folding, folding. In this light, all his hats look like boats.

Acknowledgments

Thanks to the following journals and their editorial staffs for first publishing these stories: *American Short Fiction* ("The Key Bearer's Parents"), *Permafrost* ("Persistence of Geese" in a previous form and "Slippers" in its current form), *Mid-American Review* ("You Were Raised by a Dragon. What Was It Like?"), *Monkeybicycle* ("An Imaginary Number"), *Lost Balloon* ("Everyone Fails"), *Versal* ("What Is Solid"), *Baltimore Review* ("Clockwork Girl at the Opera"), *The Sow's Ear Poetry Review* ("Two Mermaids" in a previous form), and *Quarterly West* ("Paper Hats"). Thanks, too, to Mythic Picnic and Malarkey Books for reprinting "The Key Bearer's Parents" in their anthology *Teacher Voice*, and to Michael Martone, Meg Pokrass, and Gary Fincke for including "An Imaginary Number" in *Best Microfiction 2020*.

"The Key Bearer's Parents" owes debts of inspiration to the *Barrelhouse* "Stupid Idea Junk Drawer" for the writing prompt "clown parents are disappointed in their non-clown adolescent," and to the *Book Fight!* podcast. In an episode devoted to writing prompts, Tom McAllister had found a prompt that suggested writing a story that ended with the line "Money is the root of all evil, and a man needs roots." As he and Mike Ingram discussed how ridiculous and unhelpful a prompt it was, I couldn't help but agree and decided I'd better take it as a challenge. Wanting to up the ante for what was now a kind of "found fiction" and create an homage to a podcast I love, I gave myself the additional challenge to weave in some of my favorite lines from recent episodes, including "A professional what?" and "No one should be so angry wearing white shorts." Thank you, Mike and Tom, for your weekly dose of intelligence, wit, and wordplay.

Massive, enormous, gigantic, unending thanks to Ross White, Noah Stetzer, Julia Ridley Smith, and the whole team at Bull City Press, who made this book and made it better.

Most importantly, thank you to my husband and children for their patience during the writing and revision of these stories. You inspire me.

About the Author

Siân Griffiths lives in Ogden, Utah, where she directs the graduate program in English at Weber State University. Her work has appeared in *The Georgia Review, Cincinnati Review, American Short Fiction, Ninth Letter, Indiana Review,* and *The Rumpus,* among other publications. Her debut novel, *Borrowed Horses* (New Rivers Press), was a semifinalist for the 2014 VCU Cabell First Novelist Award. Currently, she reads fiction as part of the editorial team at *Barrelhouse.* For more information, please visit sbgriffiths.com and follow her on Twitter @borrowedhorses.

Also by Siân Griffiths

Borrowed Horses

Scrapple